THIS BLOOMSBURY BOOK

BELONGS TO

....

For Les Girls, who dance and sing
and wear pretty things

Text and illustrations copyright © 2005 by Niki Daly
Hand-lettering by Andrew van der Merwe

Published in the U.K. by Frances Lincoln, Ltd., in 2005
4 Torriano Mews, Torriano Avenue, London NW5 2RZ
Published in the U.S. by Bloomsbury U.S.A. Children's Books in 2005
175 Fifth Avenue, New York, NY 10010
Paperback edition published in 2007
Distributed to the trade by Holtzbrinck Publishers

Typeset in Myriad Tilt
The art was drawn by hand using pencil and ballpoint pen and colored and tonally enhanced by Corel PhotoPaint

The Library of Congress has cataloged the hardcover edition as follows:
Daly, Niki.
Ruby sings the blues / story and pictures by Niki Daly.
p. cm.
Summary: Ruby's loud voice annoys everyone around her, until she learns to control her volume with the help
of her new jazz musician friends.
ISBN-10: 1-58234-995-9 • ISBN-13: 978-1-58234-995-4 (hardcover)
[1. Voice—Fiction. 2. Jazz—Fiction.] I. Title.
PZ7.D1715Ru 2005   [E]—dc22   2004054457

ISBN-10: 1-59990-029-7 • ISBN-13: 978-1-59990-029-2 (paperback)

Printed in China
10 9 8 7 6 5 4 3 2 1

Ruby Sings the
BLUES

STORY & PICTURES
by Niki Daly

BLOOMSBURY
CHILDREN'S
BOOKS

Ruby was loud ... very loud.
When she hollered down the street,
the man on the top floor yelled,
"Keep it down, Loud-mouth! I'm trying to sleep!"

Hi, everybo

The student on the middle floor shouted, "Hey, Boom-box! I can't hear myself think!"

The saxophonist and the jazz singer in the basement looked at each other. "Awesome!" they said.

dy—I'm home!

At home, Ruby's parents tried to stay calm.
"Ruby, dear," they said, "do you think you could
be a bit quieter?"

"Just a teensy bit down," said Ruby's father.

"Better!" they said. "Now, do you think you can keep it like that?"

But in class, Ruby was loud.
Head-splittingly loud.

Hey, Miss Night, may I answer that qu

ngaadle,

estion?

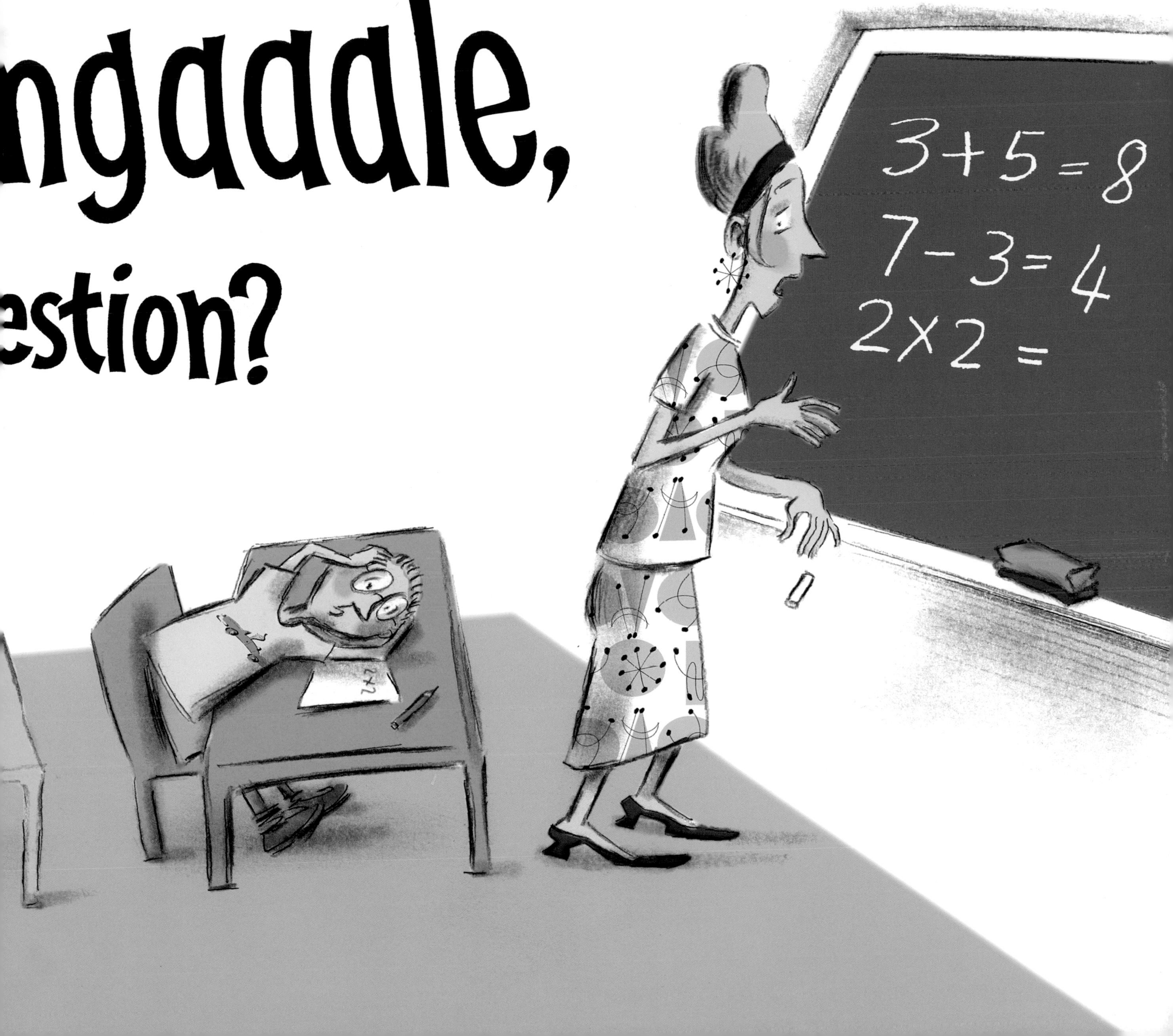

At playtime, Miss Nightingale spoke gently to Ruby. "Let's pretend that you're a sound-blaster," said Miss Nightingale, pointing to three buttons on Ruby's blouse. "This button is your 'on' button, this one is your 'off' button, and the one in the middle is your volume control."

Miss Nightingale gave Ruby's middle button a twiddle. "Okay, let's hear you, Ruby," she said.

Am I on now?

"You are always on, Ruby, and always loud," said Miss Nightingale. "Why don't we turn down the volume a bit more?"

Is this better?

"Much better, Ruby. Now, go and play!" said Miss Nightingale.

Ruby ran outside, turned her volume control right up,
and blasted across the playground:

I'm a sou

The other children couldn't bear it. They all turned
around and shouted, "Switch it off, Ruby!
You're hurting our ears!"

No one wanted to play with Ruby.
She was just too loud to have around.

Switched-off and sad, Ruby walked home.

No one in her neighborhood even knew she had come home.

That whole afternoon, Ruby kept quiet.

Her mother wondered if she were sick.

But Ruby wasn't sick. She had the blues.

When the sax player and the jazz singer didn't hear Ruby upstairs,
they knocked on the door and asked, "What's up, Ruby?"
In a teensy voice, Ruby explained how nobody wanted
to play with her because she was too loud.

"Well, we think you have an awesome voice,"
said Bernard, the sax player.

"Yes," said Zelda, "I'd love to teach you how to use it."

"Would you like to learn how to sing, Ruby?" asked her mother.

Ruby's mother smiled. There was nothing wrong with Ruby.

Every day after school,
Ruby took singing lessons
with Bernard and Zelda.
She copied the musical
notes Bernard made
on his saxophone.

Zelda taught Ruby how to use
her volume control so that
she could sing sharp, zooming notes
like the sounds of the city...

...and gentle, breathy notes
like a cool evening breeze.
Most of all, she taught Ruby
to sing with feeling.

When the man on the top floor
heard Ruby, he said, "What a beautiful voice!"
The student on the middle floor said, "Cool, man!"
The kids on the block came out and danced on the sidewalk,
chanting, "Go, Ruby, go!" And Bernard looked at Zelda and said,
"Listen, Ruby's singing the blues."

And when Ruby sang
at her school concert, she was...

. . . well, just AWESOME.

But once in a while,
when the neighbors least expect it,
she turns it right up...

Hi, everybody

. . . just to check that her volume control is still working.

NIKI DALY's first book, *The Little Girl Who Lived Down the Road*, won a British Arts Council Illustration Award. It was followed by *Not So Fast Songololo*, which won a Parents' Choice Award. In 1995, *All the Magic in the World* won an IBBY Honours Award and *Why the Sun and Moon Live in the Sky* was chosen by the *New York Times Book Review* as a Best Illustrated Children's Book. Niki was born in Cape Town, South Africa, where he lives with his family.